THE
NEW YORKER
PORKER

Written by Susie Fasbinder
Illustrated by George Fasbinder

There's a pig that lives on 19th street.
He's the kind of New Yorker
you'd like to meet.

He eats a bagel from "Ess- A- Bagel"
everyday at nine.

He watches his cousin get kicked
on the 50 yard line.

He plays games on his mac and
checks out all the deals.

He meditates and luxuriates with soaps
he bought from "Kiehls"...

Lunch is delivered
from Little Italy,
the best pasta
without a doubt.

But then taking out
his garbage,
he gets himself
locked out.

Nervous to be outside, a pretty pug
gets him carried him away.

He ends up at Madison Square Garden,
"Oh, this is my lucky day!"

He passes the United Nations
as he heads downtown.

He hops on the Staten Island Ferry,
then sings from the lady's crown.

He stops to snack at "Katz's"
on a lean pastrami and rye.

He stands on the subway platform
as the trains go whizzing by.

He catches the 'D' train to Coney Island,
where his dreams come true.

CONEY ISLAND

He stuffs down lobster rolls and hot dogs
and actually turns blue.

He's chased over the Brooklyn Bridge,
no time for dumplings in Chinatown.

He somehow ends up leading,
in the New York Mar-a-thon.

He arrives at the
Central Park zoo
and hides
inside a bush.

Two little girls
put him in a stroller
and give him
a giant push!!

He lands in Central Park lake, which isn't any fun.
An angry mother honks, "Hey! pig you better run"!

He runs by the New York Public Library,
where the lions give him a hunch.

The N.Y.P.D. show up and throw
the pig into the pokie.

N.Y.
Animal Shelter

Four hours and twenty minutes later,
he's finally okie dokie.

So good night to the pig on 19th street.
Whose New York adventure was quite a corker.
All agree he's earned the official title.
He's the real New Yorker Porker.

THE END

The Real New Yorker Porker...

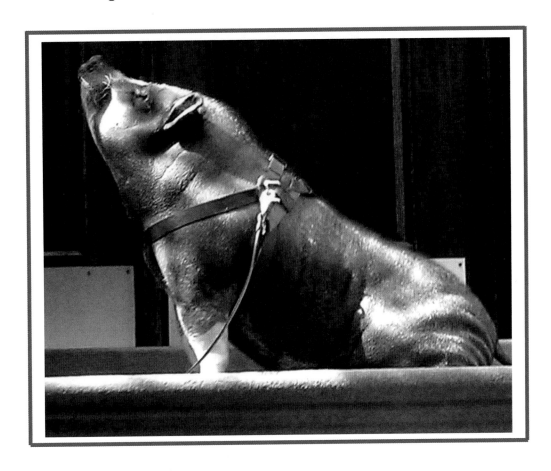

How many
New York City sites
have you visited

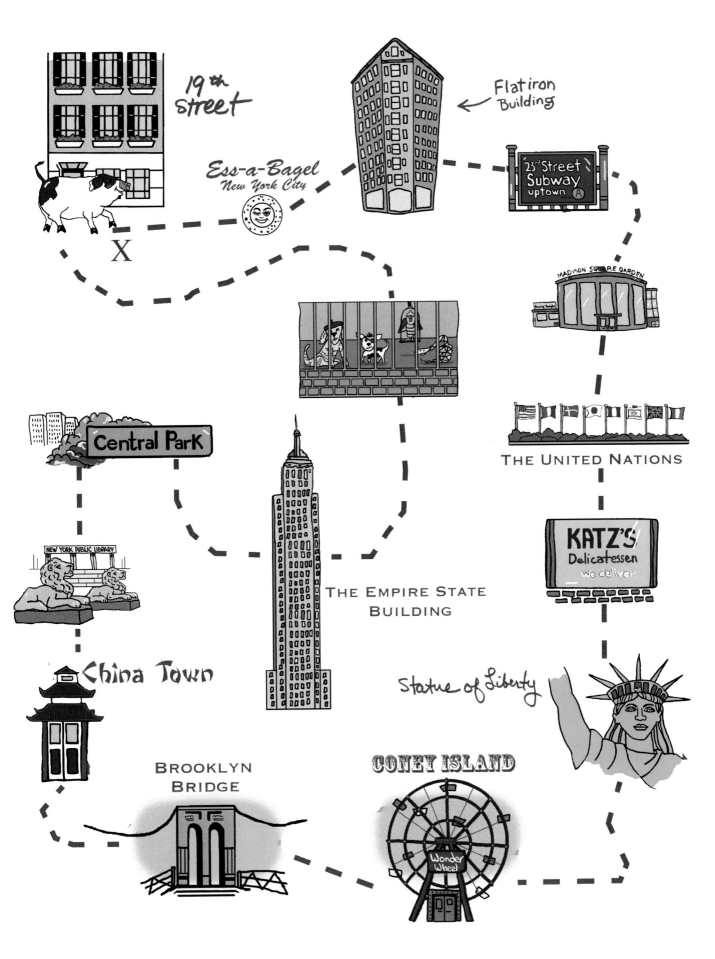

Made in the USA
Las Vegas, NV
25 February 2024

86044206R00017